Dear Mum, Don't Panic!

TALES TO TERRIFY YOUR PARENTS

Dear Mum, Don't Panic!

TALES TO TERRIFY YOUR PARENTS

EDITED BY TONY BRADMAN

Illustrated by Stephen Lewis

MAMMOTH

First published in Great Britain 1995
by Methuen Children's Books Ltd
Published 1996 by Mammoth
an imprint of Reed International Books Ltd
Michelin House, 81 Fulham Road, London SW3 6RB
and Auckland, Melbourne, Singapore and Toronto

Contents

Monday's Child

Monday's child won't eat his food,
Tuesday's child is loud and rude;
Wednesday's child is easily led,
Thursday's child won't go to bed.
Friday's child drives her mum mad,
Saturday's child is thoroughly bad.
But the child that is born
On the Sabbath day . . .
Is the worst of the lot –
Or so they say!

TONY BRADMAN

IAN WHYBROW

Bad Brian from Muckabout School

'You're *early*!' snapped Mr Tug the teacher, as Brian Busy hurried into his classroom. 'And I see you've been combing your hair again! What is your excuse this time?'

'I'm sorry,' sighed Brian. 'It's a habit, sir.'

'Stop being so polite, Brian Busy!' shouted Mr Tug. 'You'll get Muckabout School a bad name like that! You can jolly well stay in at playtime and write out the school motto one hundred times.'

So at dinner time that day, most of the children from Muckabout First and Middle School went out into the playground and had a lovely time throwing litter at each other. Poor Brian had to stay in and write 'Muckabout For Ever' until his arm ached.

It was ages before all the children came into class for a lie-down in front of the telly. Mr Tug was just looking for a nice video to show them. Some of the children wanted *Jurassic Park* and others wanted *Ghostbusters*. Mr Tug let them have a good scream about it. Then he noticed that Brian was still writing. He was doing the 'r' on his ninety-ninth 'Muckabout For Ever'.

'Who told you to write like that?' said Mr Tug.

'Like what, sir?' said Brian.

'This is your *best* writing!' roared Mr Tug. 'That's proper, neat joined-up, that is!'

'Yes, sir,' whispered Brian. 'I'm sorry, sir.'

'Oooo!' said the class. 'Did you hear that, Mr Tug? He said sorry!'

'*And* he called you "sir",' said Ben Beastly. Ben was very proud of himself. He had just won the Runniest Nose badge for that week. As he spoke, he gave his badge a rub with the same sleeve he used to wipe his nose.

'Good snitching, Ben!' said Mr Tug. 'You've landed Brian in a fine mess! Here's 50p.' Then Mr Tug turned to Brian and had a really good go at him. 'Look at you! You come in here with your neck all shiny and clean. You're wearing your school blazer and your school tie. Your manners are perfect. What I want to know is . . . WHAT ARE YOU GOING TO DO ABOUT IT?'

'I'm going to change!' said Brian. 'And I'm starting now.' He ran straight to the board and wrote BOTTOM on it in large, clear letters. He turned, hoping to see a smile on Mr Tug's face – but Mr Tug was still frowning.

'How *dare* you spell it correctly!' said Mr Tug. Quickly, Brian rubbed it out, using the elbow of his nice clean school blazer, and *scribbled* BOTUM in nasty, spidery writing.

Mr Tug looked a bit happier. 'Well, that's a start, I suppose,' he said.

It was an exciting week at Muckabout School. The workmen came to build an adventure playground next to the field, so that all the children would get a chance to show off and do really dangerous and stupid things.

While the builders were there, the children did very well. They got in the way of the men, they fell down holes, they stood much too close to the diggers and they trod mud all over the classrooms. Mr Horrid, the Head, was delighted with their behaviour. He was so pleased with Wendy Wicked he called a special assembly.

Everybody ran into the hall, pushing and shoving and making a lot of noise. Mr Horrid smiled down from the stage. He let them fight and insult each other and scrape their feet for a bit. Then he took out his gun and fired it into the ceiling. All the children fell down and pretended to be dead.

'Well done, school!' said Mr Horrid. 'That was *very* noisy and silly. Now today, I have called you away from your normal fooling around for two reasons. First, I wish to award Wendy Wicked her Prefect's badge. Yesterday she did something brilliant. She lay down in some wet concrete and made a complete print of herself in the new playground. Well done, Wendy!'

The school gave her three boos and stamped their feet till the hall shook. Then Mr Horrid fired his gun again and said, 'We've had two weeks at school this term. That's far too long, so we shall have four weeks' holiday. And when you come back, the new playground will be finished. So I want you to think of some really clever mischief to get up to.'

Suddenly Mr Horrid pointed at Brian. 'You, boy!' he thundered. 'Are you chewing?'

'No, sir,' mumbled Brian.

'And why NOT?' said Mr Horrid. 'Everybody else is! Go and find some gum immediately!'

'Where, sir?' stammered Brian.

'Just go and find a table somewhere!' said Mr Horrid. 'There's sure to be some stuck under it. And for badness sake, Brian – do try to make yourself a bit more of a nuisance!'

Brian thought and thought of a way to please Mr Horrid. It was ever so hard for him, not being a naturally bad lad.

But in the nick of time, on the very last day of the holidays, Brian had a very naughty idea. 'Now first, I need to get into the right mood for mischief,' he said to himself.

That evening, he stayed up till midnight so that he would be really tired for school. He crept into his mum's bedroom and set her alarm for ten o'clock. And when he finally went to bed, he wouldn't clean his teeth and ate a whole packet of sticky toffees so he'd have something to worry about.

In the morning, he was so tired he could hardly open his eyes. When he did manage to get out of bed, it had gone half-past ten. By the time he got to school, it was First School playtime. All the Infants were out, having a lovely time in the new adventure playground. It looked great! It had swings, slides, bikes on springs, a roundabout, a climbing-frame, a zip-wire, rabbit tunnels – the lot.

Brian didn't go to his classroom. He stayed out and had a go on everything. Miss Thankless and her helper, Mrs Task, were ever so busy sticking plasters on Infants who kept falling off things. It was a long time before they noticed Brian. When they did, his hair was all messy, he was covered in dirt, and he had torn his jacket and trousers.

'Well done, Brian,' said Miss Thankless. 'What a nice surprise to see you getting up to no good. In you go now, and annoy Mr Tug.'

'Can I just say something to one of the Infants?' said Brian.

'No,' said Miss Thankless, but she was very pleased to see that he took no notice of her. He picked out the sweetest, cleanest, tidiest, quietest child. She had red hair and she looked like an angel. Brian whispered something to her and a great big smile spread over her innocent face.

Brian dawdled into Mr Tug's classroom and stood yawning in front of the teacher's desk. It was twenty minutes to eleven.

'Much better, Brian,' said Mr Tug. 'I see you've taken the Head's words to heart and lowered your standards during the hols. You managed to be the last to arrive for once – and I must say, you're looking a bit less clean and tidy than usual. Well done. Now, tell me, did you manage to come up with any really bad ideas?'

'I've been practising cheek,' said Brian.

14

'Really?' said Mr Tug, impressed.

'I certainly have, Mr Tuggy the Sluggy,' said Brian.

'What did you call me?'

Brian took a deep breath. 'Don't tell me you're deaf, as well as a squirmy, wormy, ugly, bug-eyed, sluggy old Tuggy!' he exclaimed.

Mr Tug's mouth dropped open in amazement, but before he could close it again, Brian was pointing proudly to the scene outside the window. 'Look out there, Mr Teachy Peachy Poo!' he said.

Mr Tug ran to the window and peered out. In the adventure playground, a sweet little girl with red hair was sticking a large Elastoplast gag over the mouth of Miss Thankless, who was tied with skipping ropes to the climbing-frame. The rest of the Infants were busy squeezing Mrs Task, her helper, head first down a rabbit-tunnel.

'All my idea,' declared Brian proudly. 'I also suggested that all the Infants take their shoes off and put them in a pile. Then I took off the name-tags. It should take about a week to sort out which shoes belong to which Infant. Jolly amusing, eh?'

* * *

By the Friday of that week, Brian had done so many naughty things that Mr Horrid felt he had no choice but to present him with the school's highest honour.

All the staff and all the children gathered for the ceremony and gasped with admiration as Mr Horrid listed his dreadful deeds. 'I honestly don't know which was your best trick, Brian,' said Mr Horrid, 'removing all the doorknobs, getting all those pencils stuck up your nostrils, or filling the cushions in the staffroom armchairs with conker-cases. I think my favourite was when you chalked "MISCHIEF" on the side of a big dustbinful of custard and jumped in. That was a truly original way of getting into mischief!'

There was wild applause as Brian stepped forward to collect his special badge on which (embroidered in gold wire) appeared the words BAD BRIAN – HEAD BOY – MUCKABOUT SCHOOL.

Brian's heart had never pounded so hard. He had never been so excited and proud. Perhaps that was why he made the *disgraceful* mistake that ruined his career at Muckabout. It was a mistake that cost him his badge and got him chucked out on his

ear. For in the heat of the moment, he forgot himself, and 'Thank you very much, sir,' slipped from his lips.

'It was all on the surface,' wrote Mr Horrid in the letter to Brian's parents, explaining why he had expelled him. 'I see it all now. He just *seemed* like an ordinary, normal, beastly young man, but underneath, he was hopelessly, incurably GOOD!'

BEL MOONEY

Pretty Melissa

Melissa was such a good, pretty girl. Her mother loved to take her to the shops, and buy her sweet dresses with white collars and ribbons. Her shoes were shiny, and her socks were always whiter than white.

'Thank goodness you aren't like your cousin,' said Melissa's mother, as she finished curling Melissa's hair.

Melissa's cousin Kitty was a tomboy.

Melissa was always horrid to her, but secretly longed to be just like cousin Kit, who was really naughty and didn't care what she looked like. Melissa looked in the mirror and saw . . . pretty Melissa. She knew her cousin looked in the mirror and saw the grubby face of someone who had FUN.

But – 'Don't get your frock dirty,' called Melissa's mother.

Or – 'Look at those socks, they've got a nasty mark on them. Go upstairs to change!'

Or – 'Come away from there, dear, you'll catch germs.'

It went on and on. Melissa sighed, and did as she was told. But she day-dreamed of running barefoot in mud, and playing rough games in her best dress, and of asking all those bad little germs into the house as pets.

But she was always good.

Until the Rampling family moved next door.

Mr Rampling was a sort of artist and worked at home, Mrs Rampling had a market stall, and the three Rampling children had a wonderful time.

'It's awful – they run wild!' sniffed

Melissa's mother. Her father shook his head and agreed.

Melissa sat at her bedroom window and watched the new neighbours. Baby Rampling was two, and was always covered in soil. Tony Rampling was five and spent most of his time being a police car in their untidy garden. Susi Rampling was Melissa's age, seven, and wore old jeans and sneakers to play on the climbing-frame. She looked tough, and wild, and free.

A few days after they moved in, the doorbell rang. Melissa and her mother opened it, to find Mrs Rampling and the three children on the doorstep. They all wore jeans and sweatshirts.

'Thought we'd make friends,' said Mrs Rampling, cheerfully. 'Do you want to come and have tea?'

The children gaped at Melissa, who was wearing a cream polo jumper and a neat little kilt with a silver pin, just like her mother's. Her hair was tied up in checked bows. Tony nudged his big sister, who was staring at Melissa as if she came from another planet.

'How kind of you . . . Er . . . tomorrow?' said Melissa's mother.

Mrs Rampling shrugged. 'It could have been now,' she said.

'Oh, but we're not *ready*,' said Melissa's mother.

Melissa's heart sank into her shiny black shoes.

All next day she dreaded the tea. Her mother put out her pink cotton frock with blue spots, and blue leather shoes. Melissa looked at it, then opened her wardrobe, and stared at all the other smart clothes. The only trousers she had were white, with a matching jacket. How they would laugh! She felt very unhappy.

She stared at herself in the mirror. Then she frowned, and was glad to see she didn't look so pretty. She growled – and pretty Melissa disappeared. Angrily she tore at the bows and slides and tossed her hair. Suddenly she looked just like cousin Kitty!

Roaring, she pulled all her clothes out and threw them in a heap on the floor. She jumped on them and kicked them, and chucked all her shoes out of the window. Then she picked up the dressiest party frock (her mother's favourite and the one she hated most) and ripped it right down the back. It made a *lovely* noise.

Melissa put on the white trousers. But even her plainest jumper was pale blue with a pink rabbit on the front. So she went over to her blackboard, rubbed her hands all over it, then wiped chalky fingers all over her clothes. No socks, just school plimsolls . . . and she was ready.

Just then her mother came in.

'Melissa! What are you doing?' she screamed.

'Getting dressed for tea!' said Melissa.

'But you've spoilt all your lovely clothes,' wailed her mother.

'They're not my clothes, they're *yours*!' yelled Melissa.

'But I only want you to look pretty,' sniffed her mother.

'You only want me to look like YOUR DOLL!' shouted Melissa. 'And I won't – not ever again!'

'How could you be so naughty?' sighed her mother.

'It was easy!' grinned Melissa.

She ran next door, not caring if her mother was following. Susi Rampling stared down at her from the climbing-frame. 'You look different,' she said.

'I am different!' said Melissa, standing like a tomboy with her hands on her hips.

'Bet you can't get up here!' grinned Susi.

'Huh, that's easy,' said Melissa – and swung herself quickly to the top.

'Hey – can I call you Mel?' said Susi.

'Sure!' said Melissa happily, wiping the sweat from her forehead with dirty hands.

Melissa's mother was watching from the Ramplings' kitchen. She looked worried and upset.

'They're having fun,' laughed Mrs Rampling.

'Melissa was so naughty,' sighed her neighbour. 'She's ruined all her pretty clothes.'

'Oh? And why do you think she did that?' asked Mrs Rampling.

'I . . . don't know,' said Melissa's mother, in such an unhappy voice that Mrs Rampling felt sorry for her.

'Maybe she just doesn't like looking like that,' she said in a gentle voice, 'maybe she wants to be *herself*. Don't you think we have to let our kids be normal and scruffy? I was – weren't you?'

'No,' said Melissa's mother. 'My mum always dressed me up . . . and told me to be a good little lady.'

'Did you like that?'

'No, I hated it so much!' smiled Melissa's mother, remembering.

'Exactly!' said Mrs Rampling.

Just then Susi came tearing into the kitchen, with Melissa chasing her. They were both shrieking with laughter. Melissa's mother knew she had never seen Melissa look so happy.

As Melissa nearly crashed into her mother, she stopped. 'Oh, Mum – you're here,' she said, looking worried. 'I . . . I'm sorry about the clothes. I'm sorry I was so naughty . . .'

Her mother reached out and ruffled up her hair even more. 'Oh, but *I'm* not,' she said.

HELEN DUNMORE

Allie's Apples

'You can't fit a tree in our garden!' said Allie.

'Oh yes, you can,' said Jacqueline in her big, sure voice. Allie looked around the garden. There was only just room for the climbing-frame. Allie climbed to the top of the frame and swung her feet near Jacqueline's face.

'Oh no, you can't,' she sang.

'Wait till Mum comes home, then you'll see,' said Jacqueline.

'Why didn't Mum tell *me* about the tree?' thought Allie.

There was a ring on the doorbell. Allie peeped through the spyhole and saw a green waving thing instead of a person. Then she heard Mum's voice. 'Open the door, quick, before I drop it!'

Allie flung the door open and a tree walked into the house. Behind it was Mum. She held a small tree in a round brown tub. It had smooth thin branches and bright leaves. Mum staggered into the hall and dumped the tub.

'Ooh, my back!' she said. 'I've carried that tub all the way from the Garden Centre.' But she was smiling.

'What's in it?' asked Allie, but Jacqueline pushed in front of her.

'It's an apple tree, isn't it, Mum?' she said.

'You only know because you read the label,' said Allie.

It didn't look like an apple tree. How could apples hang on those skinny branches? Then Mum showed Allie the buds.

'That's where the flowers are going to be,' she said, 'and when the flowers die, there'll be apples.'

Mum put the apple-tree tub in the corner of the garden where it would get the sun. There was just room for it. Every night she watered it and sometimes she gave it plant food in the water. When Allie was in bed she peeped through her curtains and there was Mum, looking after her apple tree.

'Mum,' Allie called through the window, 'come and read me a story!'

'No, Allie, you've had your story. Go to sleep. I've got to give this tree more water.'

'Mum likes that tree better than anything,' Allie whispered to Jacqueline, but Jacqueline was asleep.

Pink flowers came out on the tree, then died off into prickly brown lumps which Mum said would grow into apples.

'I bet they won't,' said Allie, but Mum just smiled. Soon there were ten tiny hard little apples.

'Don't touch them,' warned Mum. 'They won't be ready till after the summer.' Allie snatched back her hand. 'If you touch the apples, Allie, they will fall off.'

'After the summer!' thought Allie. 'Jacqueline will be ten by then.'

Then one morning there were five small hard green apples on the concrete under the tub. They had fallen off in the night.

'It wasn't me! I didn't touch them!' said Allie.

'I know,' said Mum. 'Sometimes they drop off like that.'

'Only five left,' said Jacqeline bossily. 'I'll look after them for you, Mum.' And she gave Allie a hard look, as if Allie really had touched the apples.

But on Saturday, next-door's cat had a fight and came flying over the fence on top of the apple tree. Allie heard him screech and ran out to see. None of the branches were broken but two apples were knocked off.

'Never mind, Spangles,' said Allie. 'You didn't mean to do it,' and she cradled the cat till he felt better. The three apples that were left on the tree grew fatter and fatter, but they were still green.

'Not ripe yet,' said Mum. 'Be careful and don't play near the tree, Allie. We'll have one each when they're ready.'

But one night the wind grew and howled and the rain spattered against Allie's window. She looked out and saw the top of the big tree next door bending. It creaked and groaned as the wind hit it. The next morning there were leaves all over the concrete, and two bruised apples which were already turning brown. Allie took a bite out of one, but she had to spit it out.

'Never mind,' said Mum, 'at least there's one left on the tree. As long as nobody touches it . . .'

The apple that was left held on tight to its branch. It seemed to know it was the only one. Soon it began to change colour. Its green turned to yellow, and little red streaks appeared on its side. Every day it grew redder and redder.

'We'll give it another week,' said Mum.

'And I'll pick it,' said Jacqueline. 'I'm the oldest. Don't *you* touch it, Allie.'

Allie stared at the apple. She liked watching it. Sometimes she thought she could see it getting redder. It was going to be the best apple in the world. If Allie was that apple, she wouldn't want to be picked by Jacqueline.

Next day Mum was at work, and Jacqueline was watching TV with her friend Yasmin. They did not want Allie. Allie went out in the garden and stood near the tree. She knew she would not hurt it. Jacqueline always thought Allie wanted to break things and spoil them, but she didn't.

Allie reached up and touched the apple. It was warm and smooth. She put her hand under it and weighed it. It filled her hand, big and heavy. Its red skin glowed. Allie wanted that apple more than anything she had ever wanted. She thought of Jacqueline picking the apple because she was the oldest. She thought of Jacqueline giving Mum the apple, and Mum smiling at Jacqueline. Jacqueline always had to do everything. Allie stroked the apple, then she pulled, just a little. Suddenly the dry stalk which joined the apple to the tree gave way. Allie had picked the apple!

She turned and there was Jacqueline with Yasmin. 'You'll get killed!' hissed Jacqueline in a snaky voice. Allie put her hands behind her back and hid the apple. Then she ran upstairs. Tied in a sock in her drawer she had a pound left from her birthday money. She ran past Jacqueline, out of the front door, and down the street to the corner shop. Mrs Patel was knitting at the counter. Allie put her pound and the apple on the counter.

'Have you got any apples like this?' she panted.

Mrs Patel frowned. 'I am not sure,' she said. 'That is an unusual kind of apple. Let me look.'

She bent over her cardboard boxes of fruit and took out some apples. They were a flat, dull red, but they were the best she had.

'Maybe if I polish them,' said Allie.

'Here's a cloth,' said Mrs Patel, and she helped Allie polish the dull apples until they shone. But they still didn't look like Mum's apple.

'How many can I buy for a pound?' asked Allie. Mrs Patel weighed them. They were so big Allie could only have eight. She ran home with the apples in a paper bag. There was just time to do it before Mum got back. Allie found some black thread in the kitchen

drawer, and cut nine pieces. She tied one to
each stalk of the apples she had bought, and
one to Mum's apple. Then, very carefully,
she tied each apple to a branch until the tree
was covered with apples. Jacqueline and
Yasmin watched and laughed at Allie
behind their hands. But Allie thought the
tree looked beautiful.

Then she heard Mum's key in the front
door. She wanted to run and hide under her
duvet but she stayed where she was. Mum
came out into the garden with a tired face

and two bags of shopping. She stood quite still when she saw the tree. Allie ran to her and hid her face against Mum. She felt Mum begin to shake and she thought Mum was crying because her last apple had been picked. Then she heard the sounds Mum was making. She wasn't crying, she was laughing. She was looking at the tree of red apples and laughing.

'Two each, and one left over,' Mum said. 'Quick, get them off before they break the branches.'

Allie snipped the threads one by one. She laid each apple carefully on the concrete. Then she snipped the very last apple from the highest branch. It was rosy and warm and it smelled different from the shop apples. Allie held it tight in her hands for a second. She still wanted it more than anything she had ever wanted. Then Allie gave Mum her apple, and Mum smiled.

ALLAN FREWIN JONES

Dear Mum, Please Don't Panic

Dear Mum,

Please don't panic. I can explain about the mess. Honestly. It wasn't really my fault. Not *really*.

I would have called you in from the garden, but I know you hate being disturbed when you're busy with all those weeds, and

I thought I'd be able to manage on my own.

You know how I've been trying to think of something brilliant to go to David's fancy dress party as? Well – I finally came up with a really good idea. Oh, while I'm thinking about it, thanks for making the cake – sorry it got trodden on. Anyway, as I was saying, I had this totally brilliant idea that I could go to David's party as a vampire. I've taken that bit of black material as a cloak. I hope you don't mind. And I'm *not* wearing my brand-new trainers to the party – like you said I shouldn't. I can explain why one of them is superglued to the floor in the bathroom. I was trying to mend the shelf over the sink.

Tell you what, Mum! Why don't you make yourself a nice cup of tea before you read the rest of this? You know you always feel better after a nice cup of tea, don't you? And you deserve it, after all the hard work you've done in the garden.

Are you sitting down now? I hope you are, because there are a couple of things I've got to explain. Like why there is talcum powder all over the carpet in your bedroom. Yes, I know I'm not supposed to go in there, but I did have a good reason this time – and it really was a *very* good idea for me to go to David's as a vampire, wasn't it?

But vampires are all *white*, aren't they? Their faces, I mean? And they've got these long fangs for biting people's throats. I couldn't go to the party as a *normal-*coloured vampire with freckles and without any fangs, could I? If you think about it, I'm sure you'll agree with me once you've calmed down a bit. (Are you drinking your tea now? I hope so.)

Anyway, I thought a couple of your false fingernails would make smashing vampire fangs, only they wouldn't stay in my mouth. Which was when I had this *other* brilliant idea for kind of *glueing* them in place with chewing-gum. It worked really well! But then I thought I'd look even better if I put a bit of talcum powder on my face to make me look really eerie and ghostly. Those talcum powder boxes have got the most *stupid* lids. First of all it wouldn't come off at all, and then it came off all of a sudden and the stupid talcum powder came out of the stupid tin and went everywhere. (Don't worry about cleaning it up – I'll do it when I get home.)

I thought you might be a bit annoyed

about the talcum powder going everywhere, so I went to put on my vampire face in the bathroom, and I *snoze* one of my fangs right out of my mouth. I thought it had gone straight down the plug hole in the sink. I couldn't believe it!

Remember when you lost your ring down the sink and you used a straightened-out wire coathanger to hook it out? That's *all* I was trying to do, Mum, honestly. I didn't know that shelf was so flimsy. All I did was lean my hand on it so I could give the coathanger a good push, and it just fell straight off the wall. I hardly *touched* it.

And I did *try* to mend that jar. You know? The one Gran brought back from Spain. The one you keep your make-up stuff in. It's a bit of a silly place to keep it, isn't it? On such a flimsy old shelf? And it's only broken into halves. It's not like it shattered to little pieces.

I wanted to mend it for you, but you told me you always kept the superglue in that locked cupboard. How was I to know you'd moved it? I was after the key to the cupboard. I know you keep lots of spare keys in that old coffee jar on the top shelf over the work-surface in the kitchen. (You

didn't know I knew, did you? I've known for *ages*, actually.) I'm afraid *that* was when I trod on the cake. Honestly, Mum, if you didn't keep *hiding* things, that sort of thing wouldn't happen. I *had* to get up onto the work-surface to get the key to the cupboard, didn't I? I didn't know you'd moved the superglue. I didn't find out until afterwards. You might have *told* me. (By the way, it was a really nice cake, Mum, David would have been really pleased.)

That's a *useless* key, Mum. I don't know how it happened. It just broke off in the lock. They shouldn't be allowed to sell keys that just break off in locks, should they? I'm sure you'll manage to get the cupboard open somehow, and I've left the other bit of the key on the sideboard so you can *see* how feeble and pathetic it was.

Still, it was a bit of luck that I found the superglue in the drawer under the work-surface after all. That's a much more sensible place to keep it, if you ask me.

That superglue is supposed to stick anything, isn't it? Well, I think you ought to write and complain to the people who make it, Mum, because it certainly didn't stick that jar, and I put tons of the stuff on it.

41

And then I couldn't get the coathanger out of the plug hole. I really tried very hard, Mum. I'm sure you'll think of some way of getting it out. You're really clever like that.

And that was when I accidentally stepped on the tube of superglue. Wow! When it finds something that it *does* stick, it really works quickly, doesn't it? It's a good job I had my new trainers on, because if I'd had bare feet I'd still be stuck to the bathroom lino! (The other trainer is OK, by the way.)

I would have cleaned up straight away, Mum, but I'm due at David's party in a quarter of an hour. I knew you wouldn't mind me phoning David's mum to come over and pick me up in the car. After all, you were really busy, and you wouldn't have wanted me to walk all that way on my own, would you? And if you'd seen the mess before I had time to explain properly, you might not have let me go at all.

You'll be pleased to know I found the lost fang. It hadn't gone down the plug hole after all! It must have bounced out of the sink, because it was on the floor all the time. I gave it a good rinse before I put it in my mouth, because I remembered you telling me about all the germs there are on the floor. See, that proves I listen to you, doesn't it?

The doorbell has just rung, Mum. It'll be David's mum come to collect me.

Anyway, I'll be at David's party by the time you read this. If I win a prize for best costume, I promise I'll share it with you.

Your loving son,

Jack.

P.S. David said the party will be finishing at about eight o'clock. Could you drive over about that time and pick me up, please?

JACQUELINE WILSON

April Fool

'Eat your breakfast, Lily,' said Mum.

Lily stared at the large lump of Shredded Wheat in her bowl. It looked like a very twiggy island in a white lake. She wished she could shrink small enough to live on the island and paddle in the lake. She wouldn't ever go short of food, although she wasn't sure she'd fancy gnawing on huge great branches of Shredded Wheat. But at least she wouldn't have to go to school.

'Lily! Stop dreaming and eat,' said Mum. 'You're going to be late for school.'

Exactly. Good. Although Mr Trimmer might get cross, and Lily was already in trouble with Mr Trimmer.

It was Mr Trimmer who was the trouble. Lily had loved school the first year. She had Miss Darling for her teacher, and Miss Darling really was a darling, soft and smiley, and she always wore long woolly cardies in bright colours.

Lily couldn't imagine Mr Trimmer in a

44

long woolly cardi. He always wore suits. And white shirts and dark ties. He wore well-polished shoes and well-polished glasses. Lily wouldn't have been at all surprised if he'd taken out his eyes and given them a polish too. Mr Trimmer had the sharpest, shiniest eyes, and they always seemed to be looking at Lily. Disapprovingly.

Lily liked to have a little fun at school. She painted pretty purple flowers on her boring brown school shoes. She pencilled happy little faces inside all her letter O's. She took her fingers for a walk along the table and up and down over her friend Sarah.

Miss Darling had never minded Lily having a little fun. She often laughed at Lily.

Mr Trimmer didn't laugh. He didn't even smile. He sighed.

'Can't you try to be sensible, Lily?' he asked.

Lily didn't see the sense in being sensible.

Yesterday she'd invented her very own glove puppet. She pulled the sleeve of her school jumper down over her hand, the cuff tucked in tightly between her fingers and thumb.

'Hello, Army,' Lily said.

She stuck her arm up and moved her fingers and thumb so that it looked as if Army was talking back.

Army did a lot of talking, all through lessons. Army started to drive everyone barmy. Especially Mr Trimmer.

He told Lily to stop being so silly.

'Silly-Lily, Silly-Lily,' chanted some of the boys.

Army felt that his friend Lily was being insulted. Army did a bit of banging and bashing.

'Lily!' Mr Trimmer shouted. 'Stop fighting! For goodness sake, what's the matter with you today? Go and stand in the Silly Corner.'

Standing in the Silly Corner was a very bad and very boring punishment. Lily tried to cheer herself up by pulling faces. Unfortunately Mr Trimmer turned his head at the wrong moment.

Lily stayed in the Silly Corner all afternoon.

'It's not fair,' Lily spluttered into her Shredded Wheat. 'I can't eat any more. I've got tummy-ache. I don't think I should go to school today.'

'You have to go to school today!' said Dad cheerily. 'It's April the First. April Fool's Day.' He winked at Lily.

Lily winked back, though she didn't know what Dad was on about.

'You play tricks on people when it's April Fool's Day,' Dad whispered. Mum was standing at the sink doing the washing-up. Dad suddenly gasped. 'Lily, mind that milk jug! Oh no, everything's soaked!'

'Oh, Lily!' said Mum, spinning round. Then she saw the dry table, the full jug of milk. 'Are you playing tricks on me?'

'April Fool!' yelled Dad.

'April Fool!' yelled Lily, catching on quick.

'Oh ha ha,' said Mum, but she didn't get cross. 'Go on, you two, off to work, off to school.'

'Dad can go to school. I'll go to work,' said Lily, but she decided that she *might* have fun at school on April Fool's Day.

Dad drove her to the school gate. Lily's friend Sarah was just going in the gate. Lily decided to play an April Fool's joke on Sarah.

'Oh, Sarah, you've stepped in something horrid. It's all over your shoe,' said Lily.

'Oh no. Where? Yuck,' said Sarah.

'April Fool!' yelled Lily.

Sarah didn't seem to know about April Fool's jokes. She started to get seriously annoyed with Lily. But when they got into the classroom they found everyone buzzing with excitement because they'd decided to play an April Fool's joke on Mr Trimmer.

'You're going to say he stepped in something?' said Sarah.

'No, much better than that,' said Michael. 'Look, we're going to prop the waste-paper basket up on top of the door. Then when he comes in it'll fall down right on Mr Trimmer.'

'How wonderful!' said Lily.

She helped the others wedge the waste-paper basket into place above the door. It was a job to get it balanced. It kept falling over and they had to keep picking up all the rubbish and putting it back. It was hard to reach right up to the top of the door, even standing on chairs, but at last they got it wedged, just in time. Mr Trimmer tapped his way down the corridor. It sounded as if he polished the soles of his shoes too.

'He's coming!' Lily hissed, and they all dived for their desks.

They watched the wedged waste-paper basket, waiting hopefully, hardly able to breathe.

But Mr Trimmer stopped outside the classroom door. He pushed it open, but he didn't walk through. He let the waste-paper basket fall to the floor. Then he stepped round it, over the rubbish.

'Someone come and clear up this mess,' he said calmly. 'Now, get out your reading books.'

Lily felt painfully disappointed. She badly wanted to catch Mr Trimmer. He didn't seem to know about April Fooling. So she tried all morning, even though she knew it wasn't sensible.

'Oh, Mr Trimmer!' she said. 'Watch out, there's a great big spider hanging right above you!'

Mr Trimmer didn't look up.

'Don't be silly, Lily,' he said.

'Silly-Lily,' the children giggled.

'Shush, now, everyone. No name-calling,' said Mr Trimmer.

Lily felt like calling Mr Trimmer names. She waited until Art. Then she tried again.

'Oh, Mr Trimmer!' she said. 'I've spilt powder paint all over the floor.'

Mr Trimmer didn't bother to check.

'Mr Trimmer, there's a mouse under your desk. Mr Trimmer, someone's made a puddle in the corner. Mr Trimmer, I've just drunk all my dirty paint water,' said Lily desperately.

'No more silly tricks, Lily,' said Mr

Trimmer. 'You don't want to get into trouble, do you?'

Lily quietened down. Then she thought of a new idea. She simply had to try it out.

'Mr Trimmer, you've got paint all over your lovely polished shoes,' she said.

Mr Trimmer didn't look at his shoes. He looked at Lily.

'I warned you, Lily,' he said. He sounded very serious. 'You're really in trouble now. You're going to have to stand in the Silly Corner every day for a whole *month*.'

Lily gasped. So did the other children. This was the most serious punishment ever.

Then Mr Trimmer smiled. 'April Fool!' yelled Mr Trimmer, at the top of his voice.

He started laughing. The other children started laughing too. Then Mr Trimmer ruffled Lily's hair.

'*My* turn to be silly, Lily!' said Mr Trimmer.

MONICA FURLONG

Meg's Picture

Meg was fed up. Mum and Dad had gone to New York and they had left her behind with Gran. Mum had said, 'Meg, I don't think you'd like it in New York. It's hot and noisy and crowded, and there's nowhere much to play.'

And Gran had said, 'I will come to your house to look after you, and we'll have a lovely time together.'

'Will we have chips?' Meg asked.

'Of course we'll have chips.'

Well, Gran had come, and they had had

chips and other nice things to eat, and they had gone to the pictures together, and Gran had bought Meg a new dress and some paints, but Meg still felt sore about being left behind and she missed Mum and Dad.

'It's not fair,' she said to Gran. 'Going away without me. They took me to Spain when they went.'

'What you need,' said Gran, 'is something to look forward to. It's only another week now till they get back. What about doing a nice picture for them as a surprise? To show them how you have missed them.'

'What would the picture be?' asked Meg.

'That's for you to decide,' said Gran. 'You're the artist around here.'

Meg got out her new paints and crayons and sat down at the table with a large piece of white paper while Gran had her afternoon nap up in her bedroom. Meg knew this picture had to be really special to show her parents how much she had missed them, but however much she racked her brains she could not think how to show that. There they were, ever such a long way away in New York, where all the skyscrapers were, and here were she and Gran miles and miles away from them –

three thousand, Dad had said – in their little house in the middle of England.

Suddenly Meg saw what the problem was. This piece of paper was far too small for a picture like hers. She needed a piece of paper much, much bigger. But this was the biggest piece she had got. She had a vision of a picture that was *huge*, that went on and on and on. It was then she had her idea. She knew where there was a wonderful big space that went on and on and on and had nothing drawn or painted on it at all.

So now she knew just what to do, and where to do it, and without wasting time she set to work. First of all she drew her house, painted green, and in front of it were the rowan tree and the rose bushes, just as they were in real life. There was smoke coming out of the chimney, of course, (Meg always drew smoke coming out of the chimney although they had central heating) and the sun was peeping over the top of the bright red roof. She and Gran were standing at the door of the house, and Meg had big tears on her cheeks, though she was also wearing the new dress Gran had bought her.

Then, about a metre away, Meg drew the airport, with the plane just taking off. You

could see Mum and Dad peering out through one of the windows.

After that there was sea, lots and lots of sea, that went on for several metres. There were seagulls, and ships with funnels, (with smoke coming out) and in the middle Meg drew an island with a palm tree on it. Then there was more sea until, right at the far end of the picture, there was New York with Mum and Dad standing on top of a skyscraper and waving. Mum was wearing her best pink dress with a string of blue beads, and Dad was wearing what looked like a top hat.

Meg herself was in the picture in several different places. Flying on the back of a dragon, Marvel, that she often made up stories about. She was wearing her nightdress, but sitting firmly on a cushion to protect her from the dragon's prickly scales, and she was also wearing a duvet to keep her warm. You could see her just near her house at the beginning, then out over the sea, then hovering over the island, and finally just about to alight on the roof in New York behind Mum and Dad. How surprised they would be!

'Meg! So you came after all!' Mum would say.

Meg was still busy painting away when Gran woke up from her nap. Yawning, she came out of her room and stood for a moment at the top of the stairs. Sleepy as

56

she was it took her a minute or two to notice.

'Oh, Meg, what have you done?' she gasped.

Meg looked up from the bottom of the stairs where she was sitting carefully colouring in some fishes in the huge expanse of wall and she smiled.

'It's good, isn't it?' she said.

Meg's picture of the house, the garden, the airport, the sea, the island, and finally of New York, stretched down the wall from top to bottom of the stairs, crayoned and painted in brilliant greens and reds and blues that shone in the dull late-afternoon light. Gran switched on the light, but that made the colours look brighter than ever and she hastily switched it off again. She was so unnerved by the picture that she had to sit down on the top step of the stairs. At first she seemed to have nothing to say, and then she said crossly, 'Meg, you are a very naughty girl. You have spoiled all your parents' lovely green paintwork. Apple-green it was.'

Meg was shocked.

'But they like my drawings,' she said, beginning to cry.

'Not on the walls, they don't,' said Gran firmly.

'And it's a lovely drawing. The best I've ever done.'

Gran didn't argue but went into the sitting-room and began telephoning someone. Meg felt tired now, after all her painting and drawing, and upset at what Gran had said. After a bit she went up to her bedroom, closed the door and got under her duvet. She had thought, well some of the time she had thought, that everyone would be pleased, and yet somehow her surprise hadn't worked.

Later she heard Uncle Barry's voice down in the hall. She liked Uncle Barry, but she didn't feel like talking to him just now.

After a bit she heard a gentle tap on the door and then someone came into the room.

'Meg!' said Uncle Barry. She stuck her head out of the duvet.

'How old are you?'

'Six,' said Meg.

'Well, that's a pretty remarkable drawing for a six-year-old. Gran says we can't leave it on the wall, but I say we can't lose it altogether. If I came round with a big enough piece of paper could we copy it onto it?'

'There isn't any paper big enough,' said Meg.

'Yes, there is, there's wallpaper. I've got a spare roll at home.'

Next day Uncle Barry came to lunch and very carefully, working together, he and Meg copied her painting onto the roll of wallpaper. Once they had done the outline of the drawing, Meg settled down at the table to colour it all in.

'It's awfully hard work doing it all *again*,' she grumbled. Meanwhile Uncle Barry set to work with a roller and some apple-green paint.

'How's that, Mother?' Uncle Barry asked Gran, and she had to admit it looked just as it had done before Meg painted it.

'Now,' said Uncle Barry, 'once the wall's dry we can pin your picture up all the way along it to give your mum and dad a nice surprise.' Meg helped him pin the picture up, but it puzzled her. If the picture was going to go there anyway, why bother to repaint the wall? Grown-ups were awfully silly sometimes.

KATE ELIZABETH ERNEST

Disobedient Children

Cudjoe and Jonah were twins. They lived in a small village in Jamaica with their grandparents, Grandpa Gilbert and Granny Elvira. The twins were in the middle of the summer holidays and thoroughly bored. They hated playing ordinary games, like cricket, fishing, tossing marbles. Instead, they preferred to play tricks on the village children. They were so 'tricky-tricky', you couldn't imagine what they would get up to next. Unlike most brothers and sisters they hardly ever quarrelled. They were too busy plotting and scheming. Their imaginations were so vivid, they were never short of ideas, not even on the Sabbath day.

For the children of the village, almost the whole Sunday was dedicated to religion, Sunday school in the morning, followed by the main service, then Bible classes in the evening. Bible classes were well attended because the occasion was treated like a social gathering; there were no other forms of recreation for the children on Sundays.

Cudjoe and Jonah liked Bible classes for one reason only: it gave them an opportunity to get up to pranks. One day, the pastor's daughter Clara, a fair-skinned girl with bunches, stood up in class, reading the Bible. 'When I was a child, I spake as a child, I understood as a child, I thought as a child . . .' She looked so angelic standing there in her pastel-pink chiffon dress, gently rocking as she recited.

The twins were not really spiteful. They just wanted to liven up the goody-goody children in their class. They decided Clara was the worst of the lot. She was a show-off, always posing in new dresses.

'Let's teach Little Miss Muffet a lesson.'

Jonah nudged Cudjoe. 'Make her shake her legs a bit.'

'We'll have to think of something to make her jump out of her skin,' Cudjoe giggled, nudging Jonah.

As soon as Bible classes ended, the children gathered in the churchyard, showing off their Sunday best. The adults stood around gossiping. Clara and her friends skipped and sang, 'What are little boys made of?'

Cudjoe disliked Clara and her goody-goody friends. He gave Jonah a knowing smile. 'We'll show them next week.'

'Yeah!' Jonah flipped his index finger in the air.

The week went by, Sunday came round, and still the twins couldn't think of a way to scare Clara. It was breakfast time and Granny Elvira (a plump lady, wearing a plaid head-tie) was doing a fry-up. There was a delicious smell in the kitchen.

Grandpa Gilbert was a skinny man. He had mislaid his false teeth. He was always criticising the twins. He was the one who had to pacify angry parents and upset children. He stood by the fireside smacking his lips, lisping, 'I fancy a fry dumpling on

my plate right now, El-Elvira.'

'I don't want you battering up your gums, Gilbert,' Granny Elvira said. 'You know you can't eat dumplings properly without your bottom plate.'

'Kiff, kiff . . .' the twins giggled. They sat at the oak table, toying with their slingshots. Next minute, their eyes were glued to something crawling down the wall.

'Are you thinking what I'm thinking?' Jonah smiled.

'Yeah!' Cudjoe aimed his slingshot.

'Whoosh!' They fired their slingshots. Two kidney beans bounced off the wall, startling a black polly lizard. It jumped sideways, almost landing in the frying pan.

'But see yah!' Granny Elvira grabbed the frying pan. 'Polly lizard trying to jump in the fire.'

'Boyce,' Grandpa Gilbert lisped, 'my br-breakfast could have been ruined. You two always act before you think! I will not tolerate dis-disobedient children in this kitchen.'

Cudjoe and Jonah made to leave the table. Granny Elvira said, 'Sit down, boys. Where do you think you're going?'

'Gramps just said he didn't want disobedient children in the kitchen, Granny, so we are going outside.'

'You likkle scamps!' Grandpa Gilbert snapped. 'Sit down and st-stop twisting my words.'

'How do you twist words, Gramps?' the twins asked.

'Not another word.' Granny Elvira dished out the breakfast. 'You boys are always misinterpreting every word you hear.'

That Sunday evening, Cudjoe and Jonah attended Bible classes. The reading commenced with the story of David and Goliath. They admired David: he slew Goliath with a slingshot. They decided that a slingshot was a holy weapon. They regretted not taking their slingshots to church. After the classes were dismissed, all the boys gathered in the churchyard, swapping marbles.

'What are little girls made of?' the girls sang and showed off their pretty frocks.

'Hm.' Cudjoe slipped a hand into his pocket and brought out a matchbox. He approached Clara and as quick as a flash he dropped something down her back. She scratched and wriggled until the thing fell on the ground and scurried away.

'Daddy, Daddy,' Clara screamed. 'Cudjoe put a polly lizard down my back!'

The pastor was a tall, smart-looking man in a brown suit. Everyone held their breath as he marched the twins over to their grandparents, frowning.

'Brothers and sisters,' the pastor said, 'do

not spare the rod and spoil the child!'

'Mm.' The adults nodded. 'Unruly children . . .'

Grandpa Gilbert was so cross he blurted out, 'I'm going to skin you boys alive tonight.'

Granny Elvira tutted. 'Too harsh, Gilbert. I have a better idea: we'll send them to bed without any supper.'

'Shame, shame . . .' Clara's friends taunted the twins.

At suppertime, Cudjoe and Jonah sat at the kitchen table watching Grandpa Gilbert enjoying a fry dumpling. (He'd found his bottom plate in a jam-jar under their bed. He was angry.) Their tummies rumbled. They were starving. All of a sudden a furry moth flew into the kitchen and buzzed around the kerosene lamp. The twins lunged after it.

Granny Elvira wagged a finger. 'I know you two!' she said seriously. 'But don't think about it.'

Cudjoe and Jonah looked at each other in surprise. They had no intention of eating the moth. They caught the insect and placed it in a matchbox.

Next day the pastor and Clara visited. He

was checking to make sure the boys had been chastised. He seated himself on the verandah, complaining that you should 'bend the tree while it's still young'. He demanded an apology for Clara. She wore a blue chiffon dress and a stiff white ribbon in her hair.

The twins were tempted to pull her ponytail, but they risked getting into more trouble. They stood there, gently rocking. 'Sorry, Clara. We shouldn't have scared you like that.' It was really hard for them to keep a straight face. They just about managed it.

Clara gave a radiant smile.

'You boys would try the patience of a saint.' The pastor wagged a finger. 'You have no consideration for others. You're always up to mischief: running around and jumping all over the place like fleas in a tar bucket.'

Jonah slipped his hand into his pocket and brought out a matchbox, winking at Cudjoe. He released the moth. It flew around in confusion, colliding with Clara.

'Daddy, Daddy . . .' Clara wailed.

The pastor sprang to his feet. He chased the moth off. Then he comforted Clara. 'It's all right, Princess. It's gone now.' He glared at the twins. 'I'm going to crucify you boys!'

'Tut, tut, Pastor,' the boys burst out laughing. 'You can't crucify children.'

'Cudjonah!' The words slipped out as one. Grandpa Gilbert snarled, 'I'm going to tan your hides.'

Granny Elvira always defended the twins whenever Grandpa Gilbert threatened to chastise them in public. She said: 'Come, come, Gilbert; the boys are just high-spirited.' She turned to the twins. 'Boys, say sorry to Clara now.'

'Sorry can't buy soldier lorry.' The twins muttered a childhood rhyme. Then they saluted Clara. 'Sorry.'

'High-spirited, my foot!' the pastor snarled. 'These boys have the devil under their skin.'

'Boys will be boys, Pastor,' Granny Elvira said.

'What they need is a taste of their own medicine,' Grandpa Gilbert said. 'Yes, that's it.'

The pastor misunderstood Grandpa Gilbert. He said, 'Yes, I totally agree. A dose of castor oil always does the trick. It will cleanse their system.'

How the twins hated castor oil. But most children in rural Jamaica received a dose of laxative before the beginning of the school term; it gave them a good start. The twins looked at Grandpa Gilbert in disgust.

'Let's run along, Clara.' The pastor stared through the boys. 'Good evening, folks.'

'Evening, Pastor,' everyone chorused.

The pastor and Clara went home feeling good.

Cudjoe elbowed Jonah. 'How about slipping some castor oil in Gramps's bedtime cocoa?'

'Yeah!' Jonah gave Grandpa Gilbert his best smile.

TONY BRADMAN

Dilly's Birthday Disaster

I love birthdays, don't you? It's great to have presents and birthday cards, a cake with candles and everybody singing 'Happy birthday to you' at the tops of their voices. In fact, apart from Christmas, my birthday is my favourite day of the whole year.

My little brother Dilly loves birthdays too. At least, he loves it when it's *his* birthday. He talks about it all year round. Why, he starts asking Mother and Father when his next birthday is as soon as his birthday is over! Only the other day he was pestering Father to show him on the calendar which day was his birthday.

'Is it on that day?' he asked, pointing to the calendar.

'No, Dilly, your birthday's not for months yet.' Father turned the pages of the calendar until he came to the right month. He showed Dilly the day. Dilly looked very closely at where Father was pointing.

'Is that tomorrow?' he said.

'No, Dilly,' said Father. 'I've already told you, your birthday isn't for a long time yet.'

Dilly kept his eyes on the calendar. He had his very thoughtful look on his face, too. After a while, he said:

'So is my birthday . . . next week?'

Father sighed.

'No, Dilly, it's not next week,' he said. 'It's not for ages yet.'

'So when *is* my birthday, then?' said Dilly. He was beginning to look a little cross – and so was Father.

'Don't worry about it, Dilly,' he said. 'You'll know when it's your birthday all right.'

Mother laughed. 'I'm sure we all will,' she said.

But Dilly didn't laugh. He looked very cross indeed, and he stomped off to play. Later I could hear him talking to himself. I couldn't be sure, but it sounded as if he were singing, 'Happy birthday . . . to me'.

Father said that Dilly didn't really understand about time yet, and that he would probably forget about his birthday after a while.

But Dilly didn't forget.

I'm sure he would have forgotten if something else hadn't happened to remind him. For a few days later I woke up, and it was my favourite day of the whole year – *my* birthday!

I had lots of terrific presents. And I had so

73

many birthday cards that there was hardly room on the shelf to stand them all up!

One of those cards was from Dilly. He had made it himself, with a little help from Mother. Dilly had given it to me and wished me a happy birthday. But I could see from his face that he wasn't very happy. I had a good idea *why* he wasn't happy too.

Anyway, I was very excited because I was going to have a birthday party. All my friends were coming, and Father was making me a birthday cake. I helped him make the mixture. It was a chocolate cake, and it looked delicious.

'Hey, Dilly,' Father said after he'd let me lick the mixing spoon, 'Dilly, do you want to try some of Dorla's cake?'

Dilly didn't say anything. He just looked very cross and stomped off to his room.

'Oh well,' said Father as he put the cake in to bake, 'perhaps Dilly will be happier when it's party time.'

I didn't think he would, though.

Later on, Mother and I started blowing up the balloons ready for the party. Then there was a stomp, stomp, stomp, the door crashed open, and Dilly was standing in front of us.

Mother stopped blowing into her balloon.

'My, my, Dilly,' she said. 'What an entrance! And what can we do for you?'

'Is it my birthday too?' he asked. He had a very cross look on his face.

'No, Dilly,' said Mother. 'Your birthday's not for ages yet. It's your sister's birthday today. But that doesn't mean you can't enjoy it too. Why don't you help us blow up some balloons? You like balloons.'

'I don't,' he said. 'I hate stupid balloons. And why isn't it my birthday today? I want it to be my birthday!'

'You only get one birthday a year,' said Mother, 'and I'm afraid yours is still to come.' Then Mother smiled.

'Why don't you look on the bright side, Dilly? You can enjoy your sister's birthday party today and still look forward to your own.'

Dilly didn't smile.

'But I want it to be my birthday *today*,' shouted Dilly, and he stamped his foot. Now I know there's one thing that Mother can't bear, and it's to see Dilly stamping his foot and hear him shouting like that. She looked as cross as Dilly!

'Dilly, you are a very bad dinosaur,' she said in her sternest voice. 'It isn't your birthday today, it's your sister's, and that's all there is to it. And if you don't behave like a good dinosaur, then you won't be having a birthday at all this year.'

Just at that moment, Father came through the door. He was carrying my birthday cake on a plate.

'Hurrah!' he said. 'Look what I've got!'

Dilly looked up at Father. And then he said: 'It's not fair!' and let loose with his ultra-special, 150-mile-per-hour super-scream, the one that makes Mother cover her head with a cushion, me hide behind the sofa . . . and Father drop delicious chocolate birthday cakes right on the floor, where they smash into a thousand messy pieces!

Father was cross, Mother was cross – and I cried and cried and cried. My beautiful birthday cake was all over the carpet!

Mother marched Dilly out of the room. He was crying too, now. I heard her telling him off.

'Dilly Dinosaur,' she said, 'you will go to your bedroom and stay there until you're ready to say sorry and be nice to Dorla on her birthday.'

Dilly didn't say anything. All I heard was him stomping off to his room, stomp, stomp, stomp – and SLAM! went his door.

'And don't slam your door!' shouted Mother. But there was no reply.

Dilly didn't come out for his morning drink of juice. He didn't come out for his lunch, either. And he didn't come out when my friends started to arrive for the party.

But then you know that Dilly can be very stubborn.

I didn't like the idea of Dilly sitting in his room all alone on my birthday, though. So I went up and knocked on his door.

'Come on, Dilly,' I said. 'Come out and say sorry, and then you can join in the fun.'

I listened at the door, but there was no answer. I did hear something though. It sounded like Dilly sniffing – but I couldn't be sure.

Anyway, we had so much fun at my party that I didn't have time to think about Dilly. We played all sorts of games, we ran, we jumped, and we shouted, and Mother and Father didn't tell any of us off *once*.

But I still didn't have a birthday cake, and that made me feel a little sad.

Then just as everybody was getting ready to go, I heard a noise coming from the kitchen. Father heard it too.

'What's that noise?' he said.

And then there was a much bigger noise. CRASH!

It sounded like a pile of plates falling out of a cupboard and smashing on the floor. And that's exactly what it was. For when we opened the door and looked in the kitchen we saw . . . guess who? Dilly Dinosaur, and he was sitting in the middle of the floor surrounded by broken plates, holding a bowl.

Well . . . none of us knew what to say. None of us, that is, except Dilly.

'I'm sorry,' he said, and gave us his biggest and best don't-tell-me-off-yet-I've-got-an-excuse smile. 'I thought I'd make you another birthday cake,' he said, 'to make up for the one Father dropped.' And Dilly showed us what he had in the bowl. It looked like a mess of broken eggs and flour and cocoa. There was more of the same mess on the table and all over the floor.

'But, Dilly,' said Mother, 'how did you break all those plates?'

'I was trying to get a pretty plate out of the cupboard,' he said, 'to put the cake on. But it was on the bottom of all the other plates. So I had to pull, and pull, and pull, and . . .'

'Don't tell me,' said Mother. 'I know the rest.'

Dilly was in a lot of trouble. Mother and Father were rather cross with him, even though he had said sorry for being bad. They did tell him off, but not too much. They said that he was very bad to make such a mess in the kitchen and to break the plates, but that he was also good for trying to make up for the spoiled cake.

Which all left Dilly feeling a little confused.

'So am I a bad dinosaur or not?' he asked.

Mother and Father laughed.

'You're not too bad, Dilly. Not too bad at all,' said Father. 'And now it's time for bed.'

And do you know what Dilly said then?

'Is it my birthday tomorrow?'

Father sighed.

'Dilly . . . ' he said, 'to bed!'

The Perfect Child

Percy is the perfect child;
He never drives his parents wild.
He always does his best at school,
Obeying each and every rule.
He helps old ladies cross the street,
Is always kind, refined, and neat,
Never spills drinks on the floor,
Never slams his bedroom door,
Never calls his sister names,
Never plays destructive games,
Never asks for costly toys,
Never swears at other boys.
He helps with chores around the house,
And sits as quiet as a mouse
At mealtimes, being very good.
Throw a tantrum? As if he would!
But now here comes a little twist.
Kids like Percy . . . DON'T EXIST!

TONY BRADMAN

THERESA BRESLIN

Blair . . . The Boy Who Could Not Be Still.

Blair Matthews was a boy who could not be still.

Every day, as soon as the first rays of the sun touched his face, Blair gave a great whoop and leapt out of bed . . . knocking over the bedside lamp, a jigsaw puzzle, his favourite story book, and spilling last

night's mug of cocoa all over the carpet.

'Oh no!' moaned the rest of the family, and they shut their eyes tightly and burrowed right down under the blankets.

You could tell Blair's house from all the others in the street. It was the one with the burned-out potting shed, the cracked windows, and the garden fence broken in several places.

During the summer Blair always helped out with the family barbecues. The village fire-fighters told Blair's mum that the fire-engine could probably find the way to Blair's house by itself now.

Blair also liked to play cricket, although he knew he wasn't the best batsman in the world, or even the second best. His granny said for him not to worry. If he kept practising he was bound to improve. So he did.

Blair had offered to fix the garden fence, now that he had given up training to be an Olympic hurdler, but his mum and dad said it was all right. They said they were fed up mending it anyway, and they were going to grow a hedge instead. A very prickly hawthorn hedge.

Mr and Mrs Higgins, who owned the local D-I-Y repair shop, always sent Blair's family an extra-large card at Christmas-time.

One Sunday morning, Blair charged down the stairs for breakfast, tripped over the dog and stood on the cat's tail. He raced into the kitchen and clambered up onto his chair. The budgie moved quickly to the furthest corner of its cage.

His mother put a soft-boiled egg in front of him. Blair grabbed his bread soldiers for dunking.

'Blair,' said his mum, 'be carefu – '

'Watch out, Blair!' cried his dad.

'How did that happen?' asked Blair, looking at the blobs of yellow egg yolk spattered on his clean white tee shirt. He scrambled quickly down from his chair to get a cloth from the sink, pulling the tablecover and all the dishes with him.

'That boy is a walking disaster area,' said his dad, mopping up the mess.

'A pain in the neck,' said his big sister, picking her slice of toast out of the dog's dish.

'EEEEK!' said Baby Willis, and he

crawled away under the table as fast as he could.

'He's an active wee chappie, isn't he?' his granny said fondly, as Blair rushed outside to play. 'Would you look at him now?' she added proudly.

Blair was galloping round and round the garden, being an Arab horseman.

'He must have ants in his pants,' his mum said wearily.

'He should grow out of this stage soon,' said his dad.

'He may never get the opportunity,' said his big sister, running outside and snatching her best white cotton nightie from Blair's head.

At tea-time Blair came indoors. His face was pink and he was out of breath. 'I think I'll go and lie down,' he said.

'Whatever for?' asked his big sister, in amazement.

'Perhaps now we'll get some peace and quiet,' said Blair's dad.

'It's when they're quiet, that's the time to worry,' said his granny.

'Nonsense,' said Blair's mum. 'He's probably just a little tired.'

The next morning there was a deep

silence from Blair's room. The rest of the family woke up slowly.

'Do you hear anything?' asked Blair's mum.

'Nothing at all,' said his dad.

They looked at each other in alarm. Then they got up quickly and went into Blair's bedroom. Blair lay in bed. His face was red and blotchy.

'I don't want to get up today,' he said.

'I'd better call the doctor,' said his mum in a very strained voice. 'I don't think he's very well.'

'Told you so,' said his granny, smugly.

The doctor came. 'Measles,' she said. 'Plenty of rest.'

So Blair stayed in bed for four days. He said he felt awful.

So did the rest of the family.

'You fairly miss the wee one running about,' said his granny and dropped three stitches of her knitting.

'The house is terribly quiet,' said Blair's mum.

'Life can get boring,' said Blair's dad, staring out of the window.

'Everything in my room is exactly where I left it,' said Blair's big sister tetchily. 'I

can't find anything.'

Willis whimpered quietly and sucked the
end of his sleeve.

On Friday, Blair said, 'I feel lots better.'

On Saturday, he sat up in bed.

Next morning, very early, there was a loud
crash from downstairs, and a strong smell
of burning toast.

The family hurried down to the kitchen
and cautiously opened the door. A box of
breakfast cereal lay on its side with the

contents spilled out all over the worktop. The fridge door was open and a large lake of milk was spreading slowly across the floor.

'Ooops,' said Blair. 'Sorry.'

And he waited to be told off.

Everybody smiled at Blair.

'That's all right, son,' said Blair's dad, and he patted him on the head. Then he looked down at his hand, and picking up a tea towel he carefully wiped his jam-smeared fingers one by one.

Blair's mum stepped back from the puddle of milk which was lapping round her slippers. 'You're feeling better then, pet,' she said, and her worried voice had gone away completely.

'Thank goodness this house is normal again,' said Blair's big sister. 'Now I can get some sleep.'

'*Glug. Glug,*' agreed Baby Willis.

The family went back upstairs to bed.

Where they put their fingers in their ears, shut their eyes tightly and burrowed right down under the blankets.

A Solution

Kids are born to misbehave,
And how their parents moan!
I'm sure they'd be much happier
If they left their kids alone.

TONY BRADMAN

Tony Bradman

DILLY DINOSAUR, DETECTIVE

Join Dilly, everyone's favourite dinosaur, as he creates new adventures with the help of his infamous super-scream. How better for Dilly to wreak havoc at the pantomime, liven up the vet's surgery, become a valued member of the Dino-Cubs and develop his detective skills than scream . . . at 150 miles-per-hour?

But never fear – Dilly and Dorla find the perfect antidote to his loudness – the Great Silent Feud – however shortlived it proves!

This is the fourteenth collection of stories about Dilly, the world's naughtiest dinosaur.

Tony Bradman

DILLY AND THE PIRATES

Ever since Pirate Week at the local library Dilly has been obsessed. Dilly terrifies all his friends with his pirate games – but he thinks they're great fun. He isn't so amused when he's made to walk the plank, however . . .

In this thirteenth collection of stories about the world's naughtiest dinosaur, Dilly goes camping, appears on television and listens to a frightening bedtime story.

Shortlisted for the Children's Book Award.

"a rumbustious comic tale . . ."
                                        The Times

Bel Mooney

I DON'T WANT TO!

Kitty's favourite word is NO! She doesn't want to clean her teeth or wash or eat her vegetables or – worst of all – play with boring cousin Melissa. But saying no gives Kitty more problems than even she bargained for – and somehow she always ends up wanting to say yes!

There are several books about Kitty available, including *But you promised!*, *I Know!*, *It's not fair!*, *I'm scared!*, *I can't find it!* and *Why not?*

Jacqueline Wilson

TWIN TROUBLE

Nobody asked me whether I wanted the twins. I'm part of the family aren't I? You don't know what it's like for me. I wish there was some way I could make you understand.

Eight-year-old Connie is in despair – until Nurse Meade arrives with her long black hair twisted into little plaits fastened with tiny blue glass beads. When Connie twiddles with the two blue beads the nurse has given her, something magical begins to happen . . .

A hilarious and comforting story about the arrival of twins in the family by the author of *The Suitcase Kid*, winner of the Children's Book Award.

"entertaining enough to be enjoyed by all . . ."
                    School Librarian

A Selected List of Fiction from Mammoth

While every effort is made to keep prices low, it is sometimes necessary to increase prices at short notice. Mandarin Paperbacks reserves the right to show new retail prices on covers which may differ from those previously advertised in the text or elsewhere.

The prices shown below were correct at the time of going to press.

☐	7497 1421 2	**Betsey Biggalow is Here!**	Malorie Blackman	£2.99
☐	7497 0366 0	**Dilly the Dinosaur**	Tony Bradman	£2.99
☐	7497 0137 4	**Flat Stanley**	Jeff Brown	£2.99
☐	7497 0983 9	**The Real Tilly Beany**	Annie Dalton	£2.99
☐	7497 0592 2	**The Peacock Garden**	Anita Desai	£2.99
☐	7497 0054 8	**My Naughty Little Sister**	Dorothy Edwards	£2.99
☐	7497 0723 2	**The Little Prince (colour ed.)**	A. Saint-Exupery	£3.99
☐	7497 0305 9	**Bill's New Frock**	Anne Fine	£2.99
☐	7497 1718 1	**My Grandmother's Stories**	Adèle Geras	£2.99
☐	7497 0041 6	**The Quiet Pirate**	Andrew Matthews	£2.99
☐	7497 1930 3	**The Jessame Stories**	Julia Jarman	£2.99
☐	7497 0420 9	**I Don't Want To!**	Bel Mooney	£2.99
☐	7497 1496 4	**Miss Bianca in the Orient**	Margery Sharp	£2.99
☐	7497 0048 3	**Friends and Brothers**	Dick King Smith	£2.99
☐	7497 0795 X	**Owl Who Was Afraid of the Dark**	Jill Tomlinson	£2.99
☐	7497 0915 4	**Little Red Fox Stories**	Alison Uttley	£2.99

All these books are available at your bookshop or newsagent, or can be ordered direct from the address below. Just tick the titles you want and fill in the form below.

Cash Sales Department, PO Box 5, Rushden, Northants NN10 6YX.
Fax: 01933 414047 : Phone: 01933 414000.

Please send cheque, payable to 'Reed Book Services Ltd.', or postal order for purchase price quoted and allow the following for postage and packing:

£1.00 for the first book, 50p for the second; **FREE POSTAGE AND PACKING FOR THREE BOOKS OR MORE PER ORDER.**

NAME (Block letters) ....

ADDRESS ....

....

☐ I enclose my remittance for ....

☐ I wish to pay by Access/Visa Card Number

Expiry Date

Signature ....

Please quote our reference: MAND